Boys Town, Nebraska

PAUSE POWER

Learning to stay calm when your buttons get pushed

*To my parents:
Thank you for your love and encouragement,
and for showing me the magic of books.*

Written by **JENNIFER LAW**

Illustrated by **BRIAN MARTIN**

Pause Power
Text and Illustrations Copyright © 2020 by Father Flanagan's Boys' Home
ISBN 978-1-944882-49-5

Published by the Boys Town Press, 13603 Flanagan Blvd., Boys Town, NE 68010

All rights reserved under International and Pan-American Copyright Conventions. Unless otherwise noted, no part of this book may be reproduced, stored in a retrieval system, or transmitted in any form or by any means, electronic, mechanical, photocopying, recording, or otherwise, without express written permission of the publisher, except for brief quotations or critical reviews.

For a Boys Town Press catalog, call **1-800-282-6657**
or visit our website: **BoysTownPress.org**

Publisher's Cataloging-in-Publication Data

Names: Law, Jennifer, author. | Martin, Brian (Brian Michael), 1978- illustrator.

Title: Pause power : learning to stay calm when your buttons get pushed / written by Jennifer Law ; illustrated by Brian Martin.

Identifiers: ISBN: 978-1-944882-49-5

Subjects: LCSH: Self-control in children–Juvenile fiction. | Calmness–Juvenile fiction. | Emotions in children–Juvenile fiction. | Anger in children–Management–Juvenile fiction. | Conflict management–Juvenile fiction. | Peer pressure in children–Management–Juvenile fiction. | Bullying–Prevention–Juvenile fiction. | Children–Behavior modification–Juvenile fiction. | Interpersonal relations in children–Juvenile fiction. | Interpersonal conflict in children– Prevention–Juvenile fiction. | Children–Life skills guides. | CYAC: Self-control–Fiction. | Calmness–Fiction. | Emotions–Fiction. | Anger–Prevention–Fiction. | Conflict management– Fiction. | Peer pressure–Fiction. | Bullying–Prevention–Fiction. | Interpersonal relations– Fiction. | Interpersonal conflict–Fiction. | Conduct of life. | BISAC: JUVENILE FICTION / Social Themes / Emotions & Feelings. | JUVENILE FICTION / Social Themes / Peer Pressure. | JUVENILE FICTION / Social Themes / Bullying. | SELF-HELP / Self-Management / Anger Management. | EDUCATION / Counseling / Crisis Management.

Classification: LCC: PZ7.1.L3829 P38 2020 | DDC: [Fic]–dc23

Printed in the United States
10 9 8 7 6 5 4

Boys Town Press is the publishing division of Boys Town, a national organization serving children and families.

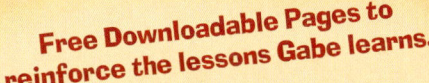

Free Downloadable Pages to reinforce the lessons Gabe learns.

ACCESS:
https://www.boystownpress.org/book-downloads

ENTER:
Your first and last names
Email address
Code: 944882jlpp495
Check yes to receive emails to ensure your email link is received.

HI! MY NAME IS GABE!

This is my story about how I learned to stop letting other kids

PUSH MY BUTTONS.

Most buttons are fun to push. But it's not fun when other people push **MY** buttons.

It used to happen to me **all the time!** Then I'd do stuff like yell, or hit, or run away, or even cry. But it wasn't my fault. People made me mad, so I acted mad.

Just like a few days ago. I was sitting in class listening to Mrs. Spencer explain that we were all going to be working with a partner for a research project. She said my partner was going to be Carter.

My partner is always Carter! As soon as she said it, my buttons popped up.

BIG. FLASHING. BUTTONS.

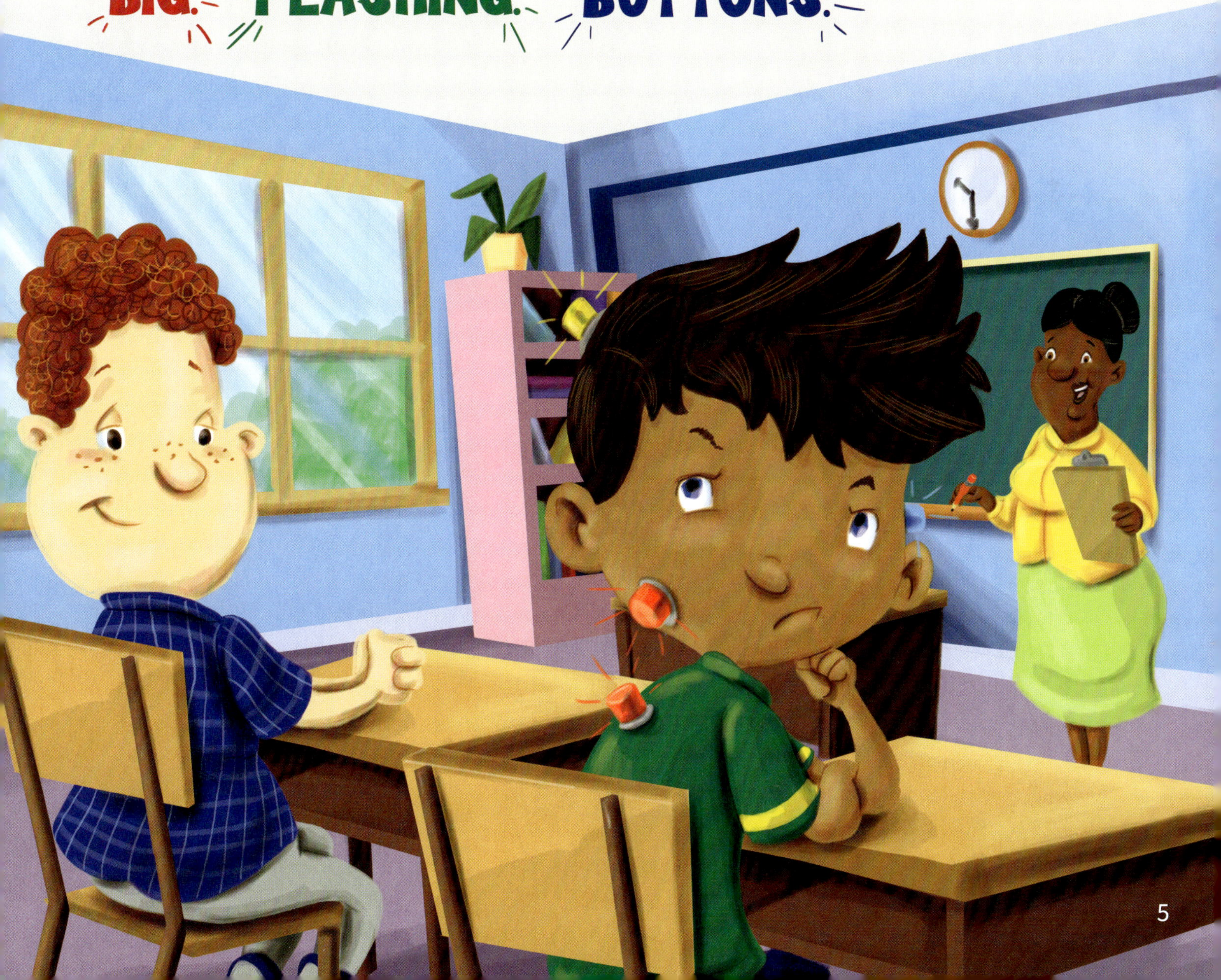

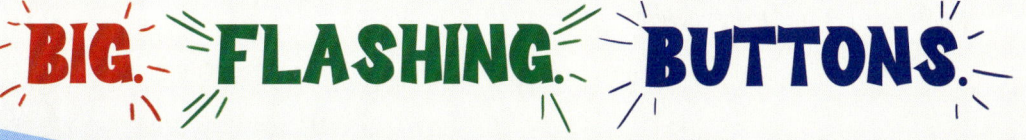

Carter hardly does any of the work, and he smells bad! I was thinking about this when Elliott bumped his elbow into me. He sits right next to me and never stays in his own space. My teacher says it's because he's left-handed and I'm right-handed, and sometimes we need the same elbow room.

I think it happens because he's annoying.

So when he bumped into me, he pushed my buttons. I shoved Elliott's arm away and yelled,

"MOVE OVER!"

Right away, Mrs. Spencer sent me to the **COOL DOWN SPOT** in our classroom. She told me to take some deep breaths.

But I didn't.

I know that never works.

While I was in the **COOL DOWN SPOT,** I saw a blue button on my arm. It had a face, and it was looking at me! It said, **"Hi, Gabe."** I didn't say anything. Who talks to a talking button?

The button said, **"Looks like you're feeling kind of frustrated. This would be the perfect time to take some deep breaths."** I rolled my eyes.

"Go ahead. Try it," the button said.

I was annoyed, but I wanted the button to be quiet. So I tried it, just like Mrs. Spencer taught me. I breathed in slowly through my nose and out through my mouth.

Then I took another deep breath. My buttons stopped flashing. They even started to shrink.

The button with the face started talking again. **"Hey! Nice job! Can you tell the deep breaths are helping? My name is Preston, by the way."**

"Like 'pressed on' a button?" I giggled.

"Yeah, yeah. I've heard the jokes before. It used to bug me, but not anymore."

"Why are you here?" I asked.

"I'm here to teach you about buttons. Haven't you heard you shouldn't let people push your buttons?"

"YES!
My parents say that all the time.
BUT I DON'T LET PEOPLE PUSH THEM. THEY JUST DO!"
I snapped.

"Gabe, that's not really what your parents mean. They mean that how you react to someone else's actions is up to you. Sometimes you let other people's actions and words bother you so much that you make bad choices.

When someone is pushing your buttons, YOU'RE the one who decides how to handle your feelings and how to behave."

"But how do I make the right choice?" I asked.

"You can pause and then decide what to do. It's called 'PAUSE POWER.'

Taking deep breaths, counting slowly, noticing how your body is feeling — all of these things can help you pause and think.

And the COOL DOWN SPOT is a tool, not a punishment! If you feel like you need some space to calm down, you can ask your teacher for time BEFORE you make a bad choice."

Preston was right. Mrs. Spencer is always telling me I can ask for time to calm down if I need to.

I took another deep breath, and Preston disappeared. Feeling calm, I went back to my desk. I worked with Carter on our project, even though he was still annoying.

The next day, I was playing soccer at recess. The other team was winning. They kept bragging about it. I felt so mad! Big buttons popped up and started flashing. I heard Michael say, "I think we're going to win. Gabe doesn't even know how to kick!"

Then his whole team started laughing. I felt like **ALL** my buttons were being pushed!

I ran at Michael and knocked him down. He started to get up to fight me, but one of the teachers came over and yelled at us to stop.

Michael and I both had to go to the office. I sat there, still angry. My buttons stayed **BIG** and **FLASHING**.

Then I heard Preston's voice: **"Looks like it's time for some more deep breaths."** I took two deep, slow breaths. The buttons stopped flashing. Preston said, **"When you use PAUSE POWER, the other kids won't get a big reaction from you. Then they won't get to watch the GABE TEMPER TANTRUM SHOW."**

He was right. I know when I just react, I don't make the best choices. Other people know this, too, so they expect me to blow up.

I took four more deep breaths and counted backwards slowly (breathe in, eight, breathe out, seven, and so on). All my buttons – even Preston – disappeared. Then I was calm enough to talk to Mrs. Waters, our principal.

The very next day, Elliott kept tapping his pencil. Mrs. Spencer had asked Elliott and me to switch desks so we wouldn't bump elbows anymore. Now I was trying to concentrate, and he was so annoying!

Preston appeared on my arm again. **"You can do this,"** he said. **"You can calm your body when you start feeling angry or frustrated. It takes practice. Be aware and let the deep breaths take it from there. You're on your own now. Just remember to use PAUSE POWER."**

I closed my eyes and took a deep breath. Preston disappeared!

Maybe I could do it. I took a couple more deep breaths and counted.

I felt calm... for a few minutes.

Then I started worrying. What if I can't do this calm down thing by myself?!

Just then, Jace threw a wadded piece of paper at me. He had a big grin on his face. That was it! *HE WAS* **PUSHING MY BUTTONS!**

I jumped up and thought about doing what I would usually do. I even imagined myself throwing that wadded piece of paper right back at Jace's face!

But then I imagined what would happen next... I would end up in the **COOL DOWN SPOT**. Or maybe even the office.

Then the funniest thing happened. Instead of doing what I felt like doing, I remembered what Preston taught me.

I took some deep breaths. I was still mad, and my body felt tight at first, but I started to relax. I counted backwards. My buttons stopped blinking. They got smaller, and most of them disappeared.

This time I didn't let myself get upset. I took a deep breath and thought to myself, *"I can handle this."*

Since that day, I've been practicing my **PAUSE POWER** *a lot!*

Sometimes I even ask to go to the **COOL DOWN SPOT** when I need to.

Now I understand what the grownups and Preston were talking about. I have **PAUSE POWER**... when I remember to stop, calm down, and think. It isn't always easy, but I know it's worth it.

Since I've been practicing pausing and making good choices, my buttons aren't so easy to push, and they don't pop up so often.

And when I make better choices, people like to be around me and I make more friends. It feels really good.

Well, I feel good most of the time. People will always try to push each other's buttons. But when they try to push mine, I know what to do now.

My **PAUSE POWER** kicks in, I take some deep breaths, and count. I keep doing that until I'm calm, and my buttons disappear. Then I can talk calmly and ask for help if I need it.

IT REALLY WORKS!

TIPS FOR PARENTS AND EDUCATORS

It's hard for children to recognize when they are getting angry and to manage their emotions so they can control how they react. It's a skill that takes time, practice, and self-awareness. Here are some tips you can use to teach your child or student how to stay calm and in control.

1 Make sure children get enough sleep. When they're tired, children get angry more often and more easily. Look up the recommended hours of sleep for your child's age and adjust their bedtime accordingly. Teach children that sleep is important because it helps them be healthier and feel happier.

2 Show empathy. Take time to really listen to children. Hear their point of view without dismissing their feelings or the situation. You can say things like, "You seem angry [or say another feeling word here]. What happened?"

3 Provide a safe place where children can calm down when they are feeling angry. You can create a space where they can draw pictures, color, hug a stuffed animal, build with Legos, listen to music, or just take deep breaths.

4 Model positive ways to handle feelings. When children see you handle your anger calmly, they are learning from you how to behave in the same way. Talking through your thoughts as part of the process is another good modeling tool. You can also model using calming strategies, such as taking deep breaths or counting to 20 really slowly.

5 Take time to teach and practice calming strategies. When children are calm and ready to learn, have them choose a calming strategy they can use the next time they feel angry. Then practice the strategy. Practicing makes the strategy feel more familiar and doable when children actually need to use it.

6 Have children take time to "sit" with feelings. Allow them to have and experience their feelings. Rather than trying to push feelings away, let children notice and name them. Let children know that it's okay to have feelings. But it's not okay to react by being hurtful to themselves, others, or things.

7 Pay attention to children's words when they are angry. Their self-talk can be damaging. Teach them to be kind to themselves. If they say things like, "I'm so dumb," say, "In our family/classroom, we don't call people names. This includes you."

For more parenting information, visit  parenting.org from BOYS TOWN

Boys Town Press Books
Fun stories for teaching social skills

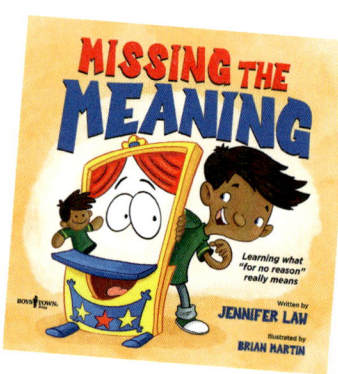
979-8-88907-015-3

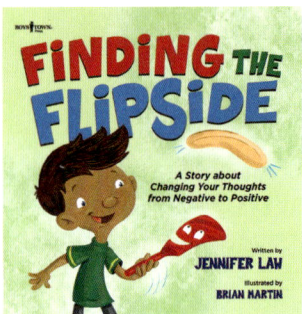
978-1-944882-91-4

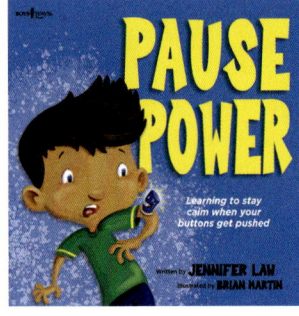
978-1-944882-49-5

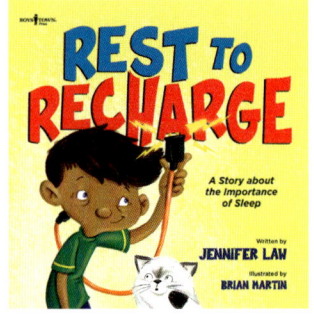
978-1-944882-91-4

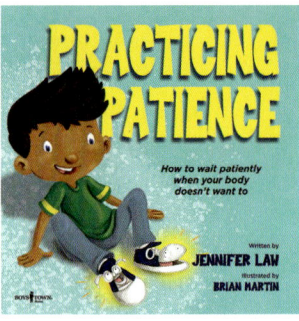
978-1-944882-70-9

A book series by Jennifer Law for grades PreK-5 that teaches difficult but important skills, such as staying calm, practicing patience, and getting along with others.

A book series by Gina Prosch that inspires young readers to embrace life with more joy, hope, and love!

Downloadable Activities
Go to BoysTownPress.org to download.

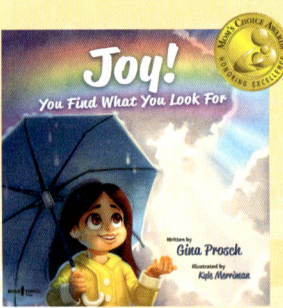
979-8-88907-001-6

979-8-88907-011-5

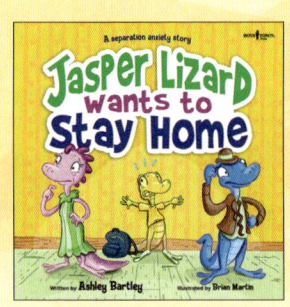
978-0-938510-95-6

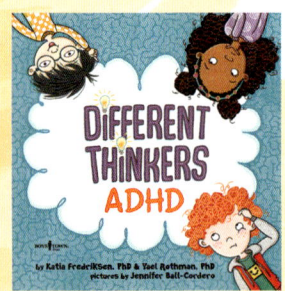
979-8-88907-006-1

For information on Boys Town and its Education Model, Common Sense Parenting®, and training programs:
LiftwithBoysTown.org | Parenting.org
training@boystown.org | 800-545-5771

For parenting and educational books and other resources:
BoysTownPress.org
btpress@boystown.org | 800-282-6657